HOME FRONT

DEREK BISHTON & JOHN REARDON
HOME FRONT

WITH AN INTRODUCTION BY SALMAN RUSHDIE

JONATHAN CAPE
THIRTY BEDFORD SQUARE LONDON

First published 1984
Photographs copyright © 1984 by Derek Bishton and John Reardon
Text copyright © 1984 by Derek Bishton
Introduction copyright © 1984 by Salman Rushdie
Design by Derek Bishton and John Reardon

Jonathan Cape Ltd, 30 Bedford Square, London WC1B 3EL

British Library Cataloguing in Publication Data

Bishton, Derek
Home front.
1. Handsworth (Staffordshire) – Social life and customs – Pictorial works
I. Title   II. Reardon, John
942.4'96   DA690.H22/

ISBN 0-224-02255-5

Printed in Great Britain by
W.S. Cowell Ltd, Butter Market, Ipswich

FOR EVERYONE ON THE HOME FRONT

INTRODUCTION

This is a book of images; and imagination, the process by which we make pictures of the world, is (along with the idea of the self and the evolution of the opposable thumb) one of the keys to our humanity. So well-made pictures are of importance to us all; they tell us not only what we have previously seen, but what it is possible to begin seeing. That is: they open our eyes. There are many such pictures to be found in this portrait of everyday reality as it is experienced by Britain's Asians and Blacks – many memorable images of happiness, turbulence, defiance, childhood, death. In a Handsworth shop, two assistants, one white, one Black, stand smiling under a spinning South African fruit advertisement. Or in a scrap of urban wasteland a child's head appears at the peak of a pyramid of rubble, while behind him rises the irony of a brick wall on which is painted a lurid scene of tropical paradise.

But the significance of such a photographic essay as *Home Front* is not only aesthetic. For these are images of peoples who have for centuries been persecuted by images. The imagination can falsify, demean, ridicule, caricature and wound as effectively as it can clarify, intensify and unveil; and from the slaves of old to the born-British Black children of the present, there have been many who would testify to the pain of being subjected to white society's view of them.

Fortunately, 'white society' is no homogeneous mass. After all, we have here the work of two white men, and it is sensitive, knowledgeable work. In *The Black Jacobins*, C.L.R. James wrote: 'The blacks will know as friends only those whites who are fighting in the ranks beside them. And whites will be there.' And so they are.

Let us say, then, that this book should be seen as part of a struggle. Its title implies as much, with its echoes of wartime privations and vigilance, as well as the growing comradeship and solidarity of the people – in this case the Black communities. It seeks to set new, truer images against the old falsehoods, so that the world and its attitudes may be enabled to move forward a millimetre or two.

An honourable enterprise; but what forces are still arrayed against it! The trouble began, one might almost say, at the very beginning:

> God made the little nigger boys
> He made them in the night
> He made them in a hurry
> And forgot to paint them white.

Yes, perhaps it started with Creation. Darkness, you recall, preceded light; but 'God saw the light, that it was good: and God divided the light from the darkness.' Then the fear of melanin-darkened skin is really the fear of the primal Dark, of the Ur-Night. It is the instinctual hostility of day-beings for the creatures of night. Maybe so. And maybe all this is connected also to the idea of the Other, the reversed twin in the looking-glass, the negative image, who by his oppositeness tells one what one is. God cannot be defined without the Devil, Jekyll is meaningless without Hyde. Clearly the Other is to be feared. Images of him-her-it often use motifs of night, or of invisibility, which is a night of the watching eye, or of sexual threat, or of malformation. Very frequently the Other is foreign; only very rarely is it presented as an object of sympathy. Two notable exceptions are Kafka's *Metamorphosis* and the film *King Kong*: Kafka shows us that the Other can be a Castle, or a nocturnal knock at the door; but it can also be a helpless bug, that is to say Gregor Samsa, that is to say ourselves. And Kong is allowed to love Fay Wray, which earns him a kind of tragedy: ''Twas Beauty killed the beast.'

However, it will not suffice to blame racism and the creation of lying images of Black peoples on some deep-bubbling, universal failing in humanity. Even if prejudice has roots in all societies, each malodorous flowering of the plant occurs in specific historical, political and economic circumstances. So each case is different, and if one wishes to fight against such triffids of bigotry it is the differences that are important and useful. Interestingly, the universality of racial prejudice is often used to excuse it. (Whereas few people would try to condone – for example – murder on the grounds that aggression and violence are also universal to the species.) And, while it is obviously true that Blacks and Asians need to face up to and deal with our own prejudices, it seems equally clear that the most attention must be paid to the most serious problem, and in Britain that is white racism. If we were speaking of India or Africa, we would have other forms of racism to fight against. But you fight hardest where you live: on the Home Front. That's human nature, too.

British racism – and by that I mean a fully developed ideology, complete with the trappings of pseudo-science and 'reason' – first flowered as a means of legitimising the lucrative slave trade, and was patently economic in origin. It expanded, during the Asian and African colonial experience, into a rationale for world domination. These are the specific circumstances without which the British variation of the disease cannot be understood. But it is often argued that those old days, those old ideas are long dead, and play no significant part in the events of contemporary Britain. If only that were true. If only history worked so cleanly, erasing itself as it went forward. If only the ideas of the past did not rot down into the earth and fertilise the ideas of the present. In the nineteenth century, it was the Irish who were criticised for their rabbit-like breeding and their cooking smells; a hundred years later, the same slanders, in just about the same words, were being hurled at the 'Pakis'. And many of the myths, the false pictures against which Blacks still struggle, date from the early days of the slave trade – the myth, for instance, of their insatiable animal desires, of the sexual aggression of Black women and the huge, threatening members of Black men. In 1627, Francis Bacon wrote in *New Atlantis* that the 'Spirit of Fornication' was 'a little foul vgly Aethiope'. It was just one of many such remarks.

It is impossible in this brief piece to catalogue all the concocted imagery and received ideas which work both on the conscious and unconscious mind to create the environment in which racism can thrive. Minstrel shows, old movie mammies shuffling and bopping across the screen wearing head-kerchiefs and carpet slippers, pantomime Orientals in harem pants, yashmaks, turbans. Yes, the golliwog, too; at football grounds, Black players are taunted with the cry, 'Get back on your jamjar.' Television and newspaper images: because Blacks and Asians, whether in Britain or abroad, more or less disappear from the news except in times of crisis. Violence, riot, assassination, famine, flood, disease, mugging: the operation of 'new values' subliminally links Blacks to trouble. Well, no, not entirely. Blacks have natural rhythm, Asians don't. Blacks are good at athletics, Asians at studies. (This stereotypical contrast is still at work in many schools.) Asians are thrifty, interested in business, naturally conservative; Blacks throw their money around, are lazy, disaffected from the state. Blacks take drugs; Asians can't speak English.

...Enough. The point about stereotypes is that, in spite of their banality, in spite of their seemingly evident wrongness, they work. They have effects. They are at work in Britain today. And they are hard to combat, because nobody readily admits to being influenced by them. Of course you can see how other people might be – but not you – no! – ridiculous. And while the great power of false perceptions is being denied, Britain's Blacks and Asians go on living in the worst available public housing, suffering from a far higher unemployment rate than their white neighbours, facing street-armies of neo-fascists, fearing the police, being harassed at immigration points, and, when they protest, being told that there is no reason for them to stay here if they don't like it; as if the ethnic minorities' British citizenship were conditional on their never making a fuss.

We live in ideas. Through images we seek to comprehend our world. And through images we sometimes seek to subjugate and dominate others. But picture-making, imagining, can also be a process of celebration, even of liberation. New images can chase out the old. This book is one notable contribution to that process, the process of getting off the jamjar.

SALMAN RUSHDIE

London, May 1984

BRIAN'S FUNERAL

The newspaper cutting is kept with a few colour snaps and school photos in a small album with pages covered by plastic sheets. The headline reads: 'Youth jailed for killing schoolboy in trivial fight'. People always gaze at the cutting with astonishment, as I did. Sitting in the faded glory of Brian's mother's front room, the irony of that word 'trivial' seems unbearable. Most Jamaican front rooms are like shrines, the curious combinations of ornaments providing endless hours of study for white anthropologists. But now I find it almost shocking to be in such a bare room, a room where the few glass animals that remain graze uncherished. When Brian's Dad smokes, his wife no longer rushes at him with the ashtray. Sometimes, as he's talking, he notices the ash about to topple and he casts around helplessly with his eyes. In the old days that would have been enough, but now he often ends up putting the ash into the cup of his hand, or back inside the cigarette packet. He's a tall, good-looking man, but life in England has marked him, given his forehead a permanent screw. Brian was the third of his four sons born in Handsworth. He was fifteen when he died in the knife fight.

'Knife fight' sounds wrong, almost as if it could be *West Side Story* glam. This was just a stupid little pushing and shoving argument outside a youth club, until one kid stuck a penknife into Brian's chest. Brian didn't even realise he had been hurt. He turned to the other boy and shouted: 'You're dead.' In court, the prosecuting QC was quick to point out the tragic irony of these last words.

'You want the honest truth?' Brian's father looks at me for a long time. I had asked what he thought had gone wrong, why one son had died and another drifted into petty criminality selling ganga. 'You want the honest truth? Their

mother spoil them. She's too soft on them when I'm not here.' Somehow, it's not the kind of answer I want to hear.

Brian's father left Jamaica in 1954, part of a century-old tradition of migration in search of work which has disrupted the island ever since the British slavers supplied more African people than the country's economy could hope to support. Jamaicans helped build the Panama canal, construct railways in Nigeria, and they picked crops in America. After the war, and especially after 1952 when entry to the US was restricted, they came to Britain.

Was it worth it? Brian's father is pragmatic: 'When I landed here I got just £10 in my pocket, and even this old furniture here,' he points vaguely around the front room, 'well, someone will give me £10 for it. So I can't say I done bad financially.' He started work at Henry Hope and Son, on a flat rate of £7 for a forty-four-hour week. It wasn't, as he puts it, skilled work. Immigrants only got offered the jobs the whites didn't want. But at the time he was glad of it. Back home, he remembers, you'd be lucky to get enough to buy a pair of pants from a whole crop of sugar cane. After Henry Hope came a job on the railways, and then even better paid work at the IMI plant in Witton. There was a time, in the 1960s, when everything was rolling along very nicely, thank you. He was earning good money and there was plenty of overtime. He even saved enough to go home for a holiday – once – playing the Big Man come from Foreign, splashing his money around the village rum bar like a celebrity. But then in the 1970s the wheels fell off. The factories in the Midlands began to shed workers like trees losing leaves in the autumn.

Sometimes he thinks back to his childhood, how every morning he would get up, feed the goats and run five miles

to school in his bare feet, with a chunk of hard dough bread for lunch tucked inside his shirt. These are the precious memories, the ones he clings to now, even though the reality has long since ceased to exist, even in Jamaica.

A few of Brian's white schoolfriends turned up for the funeral, but they spent most of the time mooching uneasily around the neighbouring gravestones, collecting names. The headstones make compulsive reading – Ali, Begum, Patel, O'Driscoll, Hu ... Here, laid out in neat orderly rows, is the bizarre legacy of British colonialism. It has the same feel as a war grave. One woman said to me afterwards: 'I hate this pissing country.' Deep down, I suspect that's what Brian's father feels as well, as he watches the men from his village dig urgently at the freshly-cut pile of earth by the grave. In the thin December light, the mourners gather closer together to sing their farewell. 'Yes we will gather by the river, the beautiful, beautiful river...' They are singing about the redemption of Black people, and although Brian was born in Handsworth he died a long way from home. Everybody at that graveside, in their own way, knew it.

England is supposed to be home for Brian's father now, but it doesn't feel like home, even after thirty years. It's like being in a suit of clothes that doesn't quite fit. He knows too that the dream of returning to Jamaica with a big car and enough money to build a smart house is about as likely as winning the pools. He still does the pools. But what the future mainly holds is the struggle to hold on to his dignity. And for his kids? 'It's too late now, I give up trying, because what good would it do me? I think the society they create for themselves ... they're doomed, doomed.' He pauses and looks straight at me. 'Because you see, you doesn't know the inside problem.'

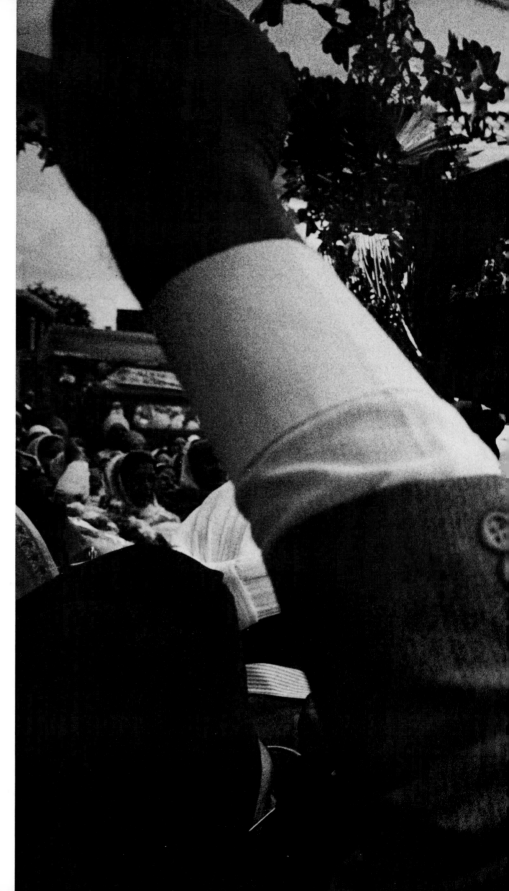

His Holiness Sant Baba Puran Singh Ji, known more affectionately by his followers as Babaji, died on June 5th 1983, aged eighty-seven. More than 10,000 people attended his funeral service at the Guru Nanak Nishkam Sewak Jatha *gurdwara* on Soho Road, which Babaji founded after coming to Britain from Kenya in 1970. He was instrumental in organising the campaign which challenged Lord Denning's 1982 ruling that Sikhs did not constitute an ethnic group and were therefore outside the protection of race discrimination legislation.

Overleaf, the funeral procession

LAY
PRAY FOR THE SOUL OF
HUSSEIN MOHAMED ABDULLAH
MUKADAM
BORN 15th APRIL 1930
DIED 21st MAY 1980

Mr Whateley was born in 1886, and served in South Africa with the British Army during the early 1900s. He was living in a Handsworth hostel when he died, aged ninety-seven.

Shri Dalip Singh served in the 2nd
Battalion of the Sikh Pioneers during
the Second World War, and was
awarded the Africa Star. His son
received the Burma Star.

Gian and his family, Christmas 1983.
'I was in India for twenty years and six
months, and I've been in Britain for
twenty years and seven months. I'm
British now.'

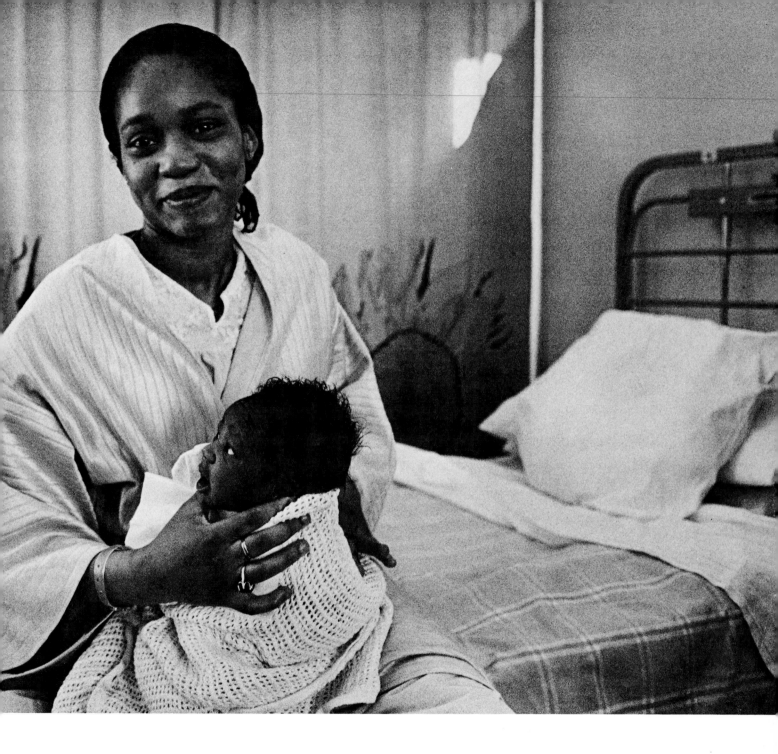

In 1968 Enoch Powell made a speech in Birmingham about the growth of the Black community. He said: 'As I look ahead, I am filled with foreboding. Like the Roman, I seem to see "the River Tiber foaming with much blood".' He received 108,000 letters of support, a number unprecedented in the history of Parliament.

THE ALI SHUFFLE

When Cassius Clay was crowned heavy-weight boxing champion of the world in Miami Beach, Florida, it was a victory against all the odds. The Great Ugly Bear Liston was a killer, a man who looked like he might comfortably punch holes through reinforced concrete. Twice he had flattened Floyd Patterson in the first round. And yet this media monster was out-punched and out-psyched by a kid, a kid who was destined to become the most recognisable Black man of the century. Twenty years on, and the memory of that February night in 1964 is still vividly alive in the folk memory of millions. The 1960s was an age that demanded superheroes and when Clay beat Liston, joined the Black Muslims and exchanged his slave name for Muhammad Ali, boxing took on a new meaning.

A boxing match is a bizarre event. Even those who recoil at its barbarity are often transfixed by the spectacle. It is as if the real dividing lines in society are being peeled back for a moment, to be glimpsed in that instant when leather greets skin. Only the poor have to fight. The gladiator buys his freedom by risking his life, by becoming part of the entertainment circus which revolves around the march of time. Every time he wins he gets that much closer to losing. Ali was different because he looked like he might be using his brains as well as his body to beat the system, and poor people everywhere loved him for it. At his peak, when the mesmeric grace of the Ali Shuffle blurred the distinction between fighting and dancing, he commanded as much attention and respect as any world leader. Or so it seemed. The truth was that he could never really escape from the white man's need to project him as the antithesis of European civilisation, rich in animal instincts and poor on rational thought.

When he tried to step outside the ring he was a nobody again, so he carried on fighting.

Perhaps that's why when he came to Handsworth in the summer of 1983 to open a centre named after him, the only question raised on national television and by the newspapers was: 'Is Ali punchy? Is Ali brain-damaged?'

The Ali watchers, who had for so long held out to us the possibility of his greatness, were queuing up to deliver the ultimate irony – Ali now shuffles like an old man in carpet slippers. One journalist began his report: 'As Muhammad Ali hustled across the Midlands on yet another incongruous business promotion ... we were reminded of a latter-day King Kong, brought into the concrete jungle for the pleasure of lesser animals.' The imagery is perhaps only a subconscious response, used with the intention of gaining sympathy for Ali, but it reflects the conditioning of centuries. It reaches out from the past, stalking Black people, trying to keep them in their place. It is what Ali is fighting now, outside the ring, and in such a contest his only victory can be to see his name enshrined and protected by Black people.

In this way Ali's personal fight has become part of a much wider cultural upheaval, an example to Black people everywhere of how they can use what they know best – oppression itself – as a means to their survival. It is probably this aspect of Black experience which most disconcerts white society. The enjoyment of Black suffering as a form of entertainment depends entirely on notions of white superiority, on the belief that the sons of Ham were destined to be hewers of wood and drawers of water. When the entertainer steps outside this role, and perhaps more importantly, when the audience realises that this is

what is happening, entertainment itself becomes confusing. It is rather like entering a hall of mirrors. The once comfortable and comforting image of the minstrel is dispersed into an endless collage of distorted reflections.

Reggae has probably been the most dynamic factor in the growth of Black consciousness in this country over the past decade – precisely because it is a wholly Black creation. It is political music in the purest sense. But when you stand and look on the concert posters in Villa Road, or glance out of the top deck of the 74 bus at the ones plastered over the pillars under Hockley flyover, there seems to be a basic contradiction. To survive, reggae music must sell itself to white culture. The success which numerous white performers have enjoyed from copying reggae tunes and rhythms only serves to emphasise to Black people the commercial potential of their culture. Reggae is a route to economic power – or at least, that's the way it looks viewed from the top of the 74 bus. But Reggae singers are selling the one thing they know for sure is theirs, and it's a painful business – selling your birthright to the white man for your supper.

Lloyd Blake is someone who knows all about this. We went to see him because he had been appointed executive director of the Hummingbird – the first Black-run entertainment complex in the city centre of Birmingham. The location is important. The Hummingbird is no ghetto shabeen: it is authentic, Up Town, Top Ranking. 'I'm the Godfather of reggae promotions in this city,' Lloyd told us. 'Prince Buster is a cousin of mine.' His connections with the nobility of reggae culture stretch from school-days with Bob Marley in Jamaica, through years of community work in areas like Handsworth, to a thousand late nights setting up shows in draughty, rented halls with terminally ill PA systems. He is in a position to understand the power of reggae music.

Inside his head is a dream, a King-size dream, of making Black entertainment the key to creating business and jobs in the Black community. He articulates the dream with such precision you can feel how it burns away inside him. The dream sustains him. Central to the dream is the potential of reggae to earn money. If the Hummingbird takes off it will lift a lot of people out of the ghetto. Blake has been in the back streets too long to give up now. 'I'm prepared to lay down my life for this,' he said without a trace of irony. He's like a climber half-way up a rock face: he can't look back.

At night, when he introduces the acts, he digs deep into his experience of raw discrimination when Black folks couldn't go any place decent, to bludgeon home the political significance of his mission. The dream is pure enough, even if the day-to-day reality isn't. And, outside his office, the problems of day-to-day reality pile up. The Hummingbird was conceived as a kind of job creation scheme, organised by the West Indian Federation and supported by a consortium of business, local and central government finance. It was set up following a feasibility study carried out by university experts at the request of the local authority. The experts, however, behaved in stereotypical fashion and cocked the whole thing up. They just didn't know enough about the Black music business. And when the local press started running complaints from Tory councillors who questioned the desirability of setting up a Black nightclub on the rates, the chances of getting more money disappeared. In effect, the club was broke before it opened its doors. Lloyd Blake knows this. A businessman would have refused to take the risk. A businessman would have seen that the only way the club could survive would be to exploit those it was trying to help. Lloyd Blake knows this too. But the dream drives him on.

While we were talking to him, the phone rang and Blake began to give the figures for the previous night. 'We got £400 up front from the promoters, which paid for the publicity, but we only got 120 paying customers. The bar did £355, which was good ... considering.' He tailed off. Basically, it had not been a good night. Then he added: 'Happily the two bands played for free.'

The Hummingbird closed eight months after opening.

'I'm saying this from the bottom of my heart – I've been to Africa, Asia, China, Russia, and all over the States, and I've never had acceptance better than I've had here.' Muhammad Ali in Handsworth, August 1983.

39

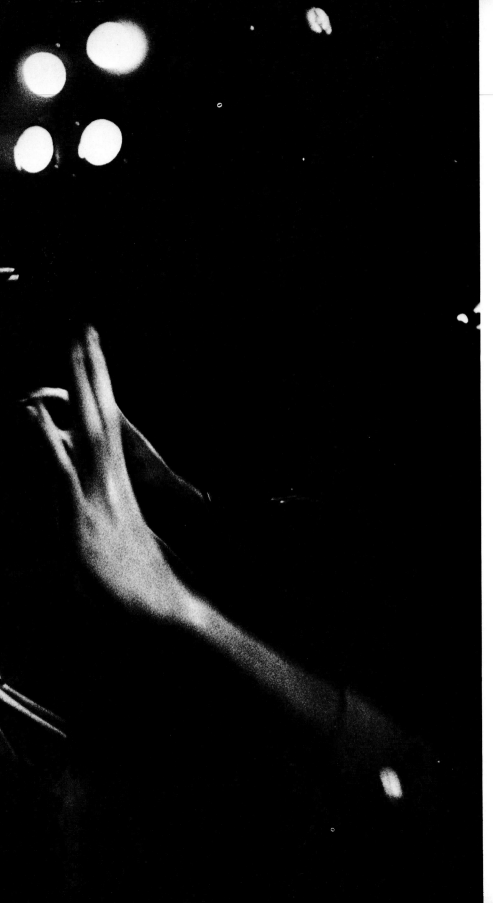

Two Tone music emerged in the late
1970s, the first multiracial response by
British youth to the growing influence of
Jamaican music in this country.
Inspired by reggae and the earlier ska, it
became the expression of a new inner
city music culture. With its fusion of
Black and white performers, it was for a
time a highly marketable commodity for
record companies – while Black reggae
remained on the commercial fringe.
Many Two Tone bands such as The
Selector (pictured) became involved
with 'political' issues such as Rock
Against Racism.

Peter Tosh, the Jamaican reggae
singer, and Lloyd Blake backstage at
the Hummingbird. Tosh, along with Bob
Marley and Bunny Wailer, was a
founder member of The Wailers, the
first internationally-known reggae
group.

Left, Radar's Records
Top, Mr Knight and his daughter, Monte Carlo Club
Far right, Blackwood, Jungleman sound system

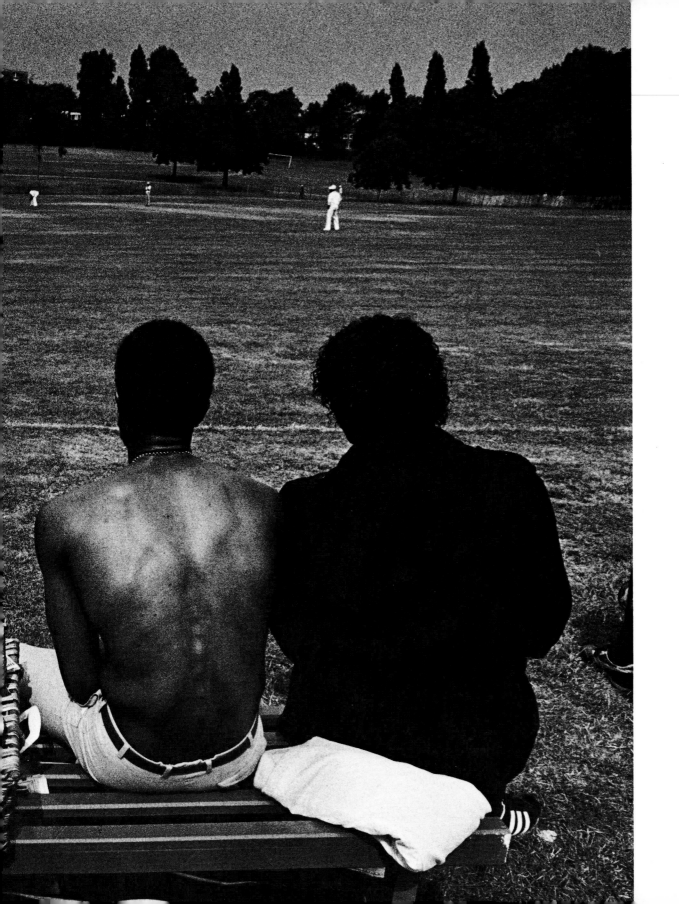

Kokuma Dance Company

Above right, Hamilton Silwane and
John Ledwaba, Soyikwa Theatre
Group, Soweto
Opposite page, Maishe Maponya

Top, Ingoapele, South African poet
Above, Par 'C', Ghanaian actor

Handsworth Cultural Centre was set up by the West Midlands Probation Service under one of its senior officers, Bob Ramdhanie, to offer more appropriate cultural outlets to young Black people. Under Ramdhanie's direction it became a focal point for the development of interest in African culture, both traditional dance and music and contemporary theatre and poetry. Visiting African artists provided many young people with the means to grasp a fuller understanding of their heritage. When a trip to Ghana was organised by the centre the *Sun* newspaper ran a headline – 'Rain dance on the rates' – and reported how Conservative councillors were furious about ratepayers' money being used to teach youngsters 'the rain dance, fertility dances and the use of primitive drums'.

Overleaf, the Princess of Wales visits the centre

THE FALKLANDS FACTOR

When Margaret Thatcher led the Conservative Party to an overwhelming victory in the 1983 general election, political commentators were fond of talking about the Falklands Factor. It was, they maintained, probably the single most important influence in securing support for a government which, in many other respects, had become remote from large sections of the electorate. Mrs Thatcher's excursions into the realms of gunboat diplomacy had revived fond memories of Britain's quite recent past when nearly eleven million square miles of the earth's surface constituted an empire upon which the sun never set. A new word, Exocet, entered the nation's vocabulary, and the millions of pounds spent mobilising our armed forces seemed like a small price to pay for the preservation of Britain's image as defender of the faith. Wave after wave of jingoistic fervour swept the Tories further ahead in the opinion polls, and it became a heresy to question the morality of the war. But the biggest heresy of all surrounded the questionable status of the 1,800 or so Falkland Islanders who, because they were mostly fourth- and fifth-generation settlers, could no longer qualify for automatic British citizenship under the provisions of the Nationality Bill which was introduced a few months before the election.

As the lampposts began to sprout party political slogans, it seemed ever more curious that a war had been fought in the South Atlantic to defend the rights of those whose connection with Britain lay in the remote past, while the rights of many actually walking past the slogans were under attack. On the streets of Handsworth, the Falklands Factor served only to further undermine the status of Black people, since the all-white islanders had been given ministe-rial assurances that although they were not legally entitled to British citizenship, immigration officers had been ordered to exercise their discretion and allow them to settle permanently in Britain – if any so desired. The political double-speak reached its zenith when the Conservatives prepared an advertisement for insertion in what they termed the 'ethnic press', which showed a photograph of a Black man with the legend 'Labour says he's black. Tories say he's British.'

The ironies of the campaign were brought into even sharper relief by the candidates themselves. The Tories chose Pramila Le Hunte, an Indian-born woman married to an Englishman. Mrs Le Hunte speaks Urdu, Punjabi and Hindi, graduated from Cambridge and, as the Head of English at a Harrow school, 'bestrides' (to quote The Times) 'the two cultures'. On paper she looked to have as good a chance as any of becoming Britain's first Black MP for more than fifty years. But she reckoned without the Falklands Factor. Her ability to communicate in mother tongues could not compensate for the fact that, overwhelmingly, people from the Indian sub-continent felt threatened by her party's stance on immigration. Even more significantly, one of her opponents on polling day was a fellow countryman, Baba Singh Bakhtaura, who was himself threatened with deportation. Bakhtaura, a Punjabi folk singer, had been charged with overstaying his visitor's permit. His argument was simply that the Sikh community did not want him to return immediately and, since he was completely self-supporting from his work in gurdwaras, why should he be refused permission to stay on? Demands for his removal seemed to many like a direct attack on the Punjabi community – especially in the light of the discretion exercised for the Falkland Islanders.

On polling day, Ladywood went Labour easily enough, against a background of Tory landslides elsewhere. The new MP, Clare Short, had been instrumental in setting up the first regular immigration advice sessions in Handsworth during her political groundings in the 1970s. But if immigration policy was perhaps more important as an election issue in Handsworth than some other places, that was only because it brought other aspects of inner city politics into sharper focus. Especially the politics of decline.

Birmingham had grown into a great industrial centre as a direct result of the triangular trade: British manufactured goods were exchanged for African slaves who worked the Caribbean plantations. In the eighteenth century it was a common saying that the price of a Negro was one Birmingham gun, and the city exported between 100,000 and 150,000 African muskets annually. The fabulous profits engineered by the triangular trade became the building bricks of the economic revolution which made Birmingham one of the most powerful industrial centres in the world. An old historian of the city reminds us of the extent of this influence: 'Axes for India, and tomahawks for the natives of North America; and to Cuba and the Brazils chains, and iron collars for the poor slaves ... In the primeval forests of America the Birmingham axe struck down the old trees; the cattle pastures of Australia rang with the sound of Birmingham bells; in East India and the West they tended the fields of sugar cane with Birmingham hoes ...' That was written in 1894, and less than one hundred years later the factories which once dominated the world have fallen silent.In bizarre acts of industrial cannibalism, old foundries are dismantled and fed into the few that remain, while the monolithic industrial estates of the last century stand, like Ozymandias, inviting the mighty to look and despair. Curiously enough, though, it was when they closed down Woolworth's on Soho Road that Handsworth's transition to a Third World economy seemed to be final and complete. As Woolies closed, a new cut-price super-saver shop opened opposite. And neither the extensive cosmetic attention being paid to the shop fronts of Soho Road by the West Midlands council, nor the legendary Asian entrepreneurial flair that abounds, can mask the imploding economics of the area.

Once, when I was a junior reporter in Newcastle, I was sent to do a story about a Northumberland village called Amble because unemployment there – 8 per cent – was double the national average. That was in 1971. In 1983 official estimates suggested that in parts of Handsworth three out of every four young people were unemployed. We are punch drunk with unemployment statistics: the figures are so staggeringly high that it is impossible to calculate the damage that is being caused, and how deeply the economic power of the community is being eroded. Even the junk shops are closing down, because people have sold all their junk. There is no more to sell. When Woolies closed it became all too obvious that all you can realistically shop for in Soho Road is food, expensive imports such as videos, and very cheap clothes.

A few years ago, the majority of those cheap clothes were imported from Third World countries – now they are mostly made down the road. If you walk out of Handsworth towards Smethwick town centre this change becomes graphically obvious, because here in the row upon row of run-down manufacturing relics is the new economic base – clothes making. One of the biggest relics belongs to Prem Singh Raindi, a jovial-looking forty-year-old with a big Merc and personalised number-plates. Prem came to England when he was fifteen and joined his father who had been working in a Smethwick foundry for five years. Almost immediately he began selling clothes door-to-door in his spare time. Within a year he was working a night shift at the foundry and a day shift at home making clothes. And when the foundry made its night shift workers redundant in 1969 – the first icy gusts of the recession that was to follow – Prem moved into clothing manufacture full time.

When you talk to Prem's senior employees, both English and Indian, they describe his struggle to establish a business in heroic langauge. Indeed, his personal story is one of incredible strength and tenacity. He worked for years without a day off, and moved his workshop from one inadequate, cramped and overcrowded place to another at a moment's notice when the neighbours' complaints finally got too bad, or the Factory Inspectorate were after him about blocked drains and non-existent fire-escapes. He once moved into two houses next door to one another on Saturday, knocked the dividing walls through on Sunday and started production on Monday. During the 1970s Prem built up a workforce of seventy machinists exclusively making Harrington jackets, which are a particular fashion preference of skinheads. The skinhead market was stable and Prem supplied large numbers of the jackets to budget chain shops. By 1976 he could afford to expand into 110,000 square feet of disused factory space in Smethwick. By 1984 his workforce numbered 350 and his annual turnover was in the region of £8 million.

Sweatshops depend on the availability of a desperate workforce. Prem's direct competitors are the sweatshops of the Third World, where wages can be kept low because there are plenty of desperate workers. To stay in business he must keep the wages of his workers low as well. In 1982, 300 women machinists at P.S. Raindi Textiles went on strike in protest at the sacking of two men who had been recruiting for the Transport and General Workers' Union. Their payslips showed that some women received a net pay of £26 for a forty-five-hour week, and even the best paid were only taking home between £35 and £40. In some people's eyes this makes Prem Singh Raindi a wicked man, but he can see only an economic moral: 'I created 350 jobs which didn't exist a few years ago. They will cease to exist if wages rise.'

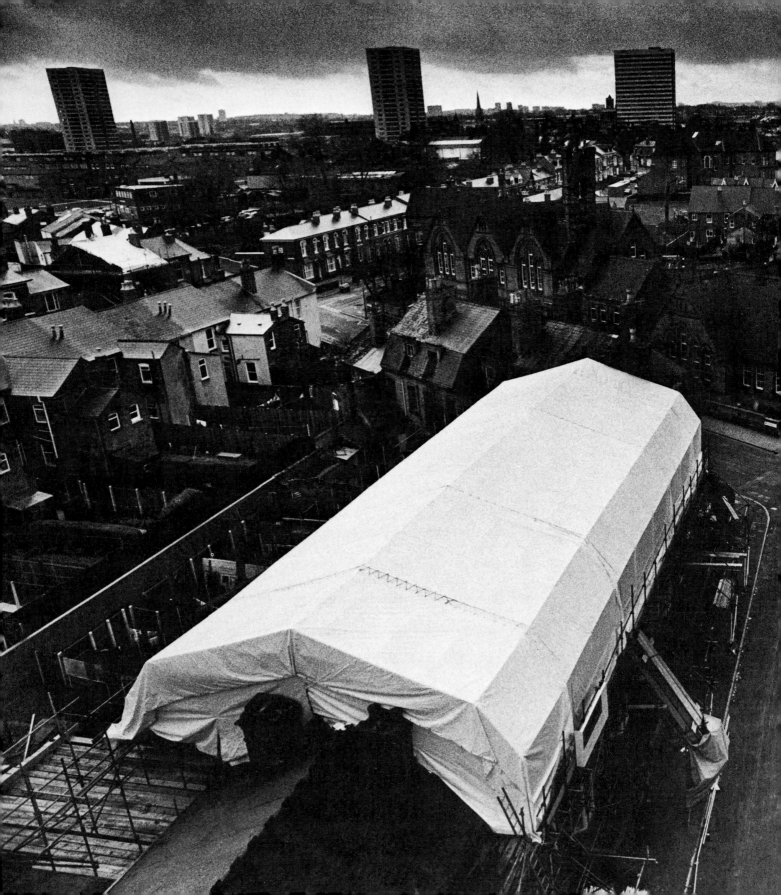

An experimental plastic sheeting, first developed during the Falklands conflict to shelter troops, here being used by contractors working on the 'envelope' scheme in the inner city. Enveloping – providing new roofs and windows free of charge – is the most recent solution to halting the decline of the housing stock in poor areas. Handsworth has been extensively enveloped.

Pramila Le Hunte, the Conservative
candidate, on the campaign trail, Soho
Road, Handsworth, 1983

Clare Short, elected Labour MP for
Ladywood at the general election

The 1983 election signalled the end for Michael Foot, but the start of a determined bid by Black people to enter politics. Gus Williams (*opposite page, top right*), a Liberal, stood as the Alliance candidate in the neighbouring constituency of Perry Barr, while in Ladywood the independent Baba Bakhtaura (*above*) gained more votes than the Workers' Revolutionary Party candidate (*opposite*).

Muhammad Idrish (*right*), a Bangladeshi teacher, came to Britain in 1976 to continue his studies. He met and later married an Englishwoman. After five years the couple separated and the Home Office began deportation proceedings on the grounds that the marriage had been one of convenience. On average, 250 people are deported from Britain every month.

Mohinder Singh (*overleaf*) was deported after a car in which he was travelling was stopped by police in connection with a minor motoring offence. Via computer link-ups it was discovered that Mohinder had entered Britain in 1971 without passing through immigration control. By 1981 he was settled with a wife and two children, but he was also an 'illegal immigrant' – a criminal. A worker at the Asian Resource Centre (*right*) where his defence campaign was organised, said: 'How can you call anyone who came to work in the worst paid, dirtiest job imaginable a criminal?'

Birmingham used to be called the city of a thousand trades. A report compiled in 1983 revealed that the region had the slowest economic growth rate in the country over the previous ten years, the fastest-growing unemployment rate, the worst long-term unemployment and the bleakest job prospects, with forty-six unemployed for every vacancy.

Soho Road, Handsworth, 1984.
'The Asian capitalist success story
is an illusion. Asian entrepreneurs
are entering not an upwards ladder
leading to material enrichment but a
dead end on the fringe of the modern
economy ...' – This comes from a
report surveying 600 Asian retailers in
1983. The report showed that 70 per
cent of the British Asian community
was involved in retailing, and that
Asians made greater sacrifices by
staying open longer hours than their
white counterparts. Two-thirds of
Asian shop employees were relatives of
the owner.

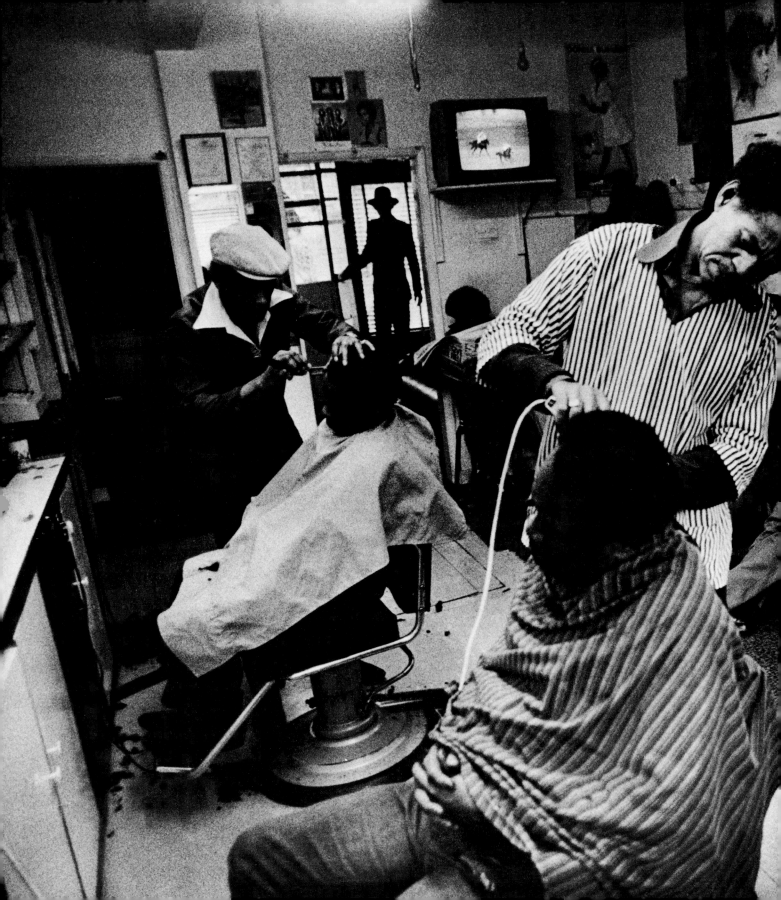

GIVE US A FUTURE

JOBS
EXPRES

In July 1982, only seventy-three of the 1,890 who reached school-leaving age in Handsworth were able to find regular, full-time employment. YOP and then MSC schemes have attempted to alleviate this situation by offering job training. One MSC organiser said: 'If you want some kids to shovel shit, no problem. But if you want to offer real training for a proper job, forget it.'

A leading member of the West Midlands branch of the British Movement – a neo-Nazi organisation – was jailed for seven years in January 1981 for conspiring to stir up race hatred and illegal possession of firearms. When police raided his parents' farm they found a cache of arms including a sub-machine gun, revolvers, CS anti-riot gas and more than 5,000 rounds of ammunition. He said he did not care if his activities caused alarm amongst immigrant groups. 'My whole life discriminates between Black and white and I want to get others to discriminate against Black people.'

Right, Eddie Chambers, artist

TALKING BLUES

The Handsworth riots were staged with great efficiency. They began on Friday July 10th, 1981, when the shopkeepers on Soho Road started boarding up their windows. Some did it themselves, while others employed crews of security advisers armed with hammers, nails, saws and large sheets of plywood with their telephone number stencilled in each corner. As the afternoon of the 10th wore on, more and more of the main street disappeared behind plywood. It was rather like a frontier settlement getting word that bandits were in the vicinity.

'What's up?' asked one shopper, genuinely puzzled. 'There's an army of skinheads on the way from West Bromwich,' said a security adviser with a telephone number stencilled on to his donkey jacket. On the pavement, next to a stack of plywood, a transistor radio was beaming out the same telephone number on the hour, every hour, reminding shopkeepers that in these troubled times it was better to be safe than sorry. As advertising campaigns for riots go, this was pretty good.

A few hours later, outside the Frighted Horse, a skinhead reception committee had gathered to discuss tactics. Between mouthfuls of Red Stripe and barley wine the battle plan unfolded: 'Me gwine mash up dem bumbo clart skin'eads tu rass' seemed to be the consensus. It was all good-humoured stuff.

On the opposite side to the pub, Superintendent David Webb from Thornhill Road police station was backed up against the unprotected plate glass window of the fish and chip shop, surrounded by a disconsolate group of kids. Webb had adopted a catchy image as the Talking Policeman, a man who spent more time on the streets than behind a desk, but it was clear that on this particular night he was in for a hard ride. Perhaps for a moment he had started to believe his own publicity because he appeared to be out there alone. No other policemen were visible, and it gave Soho Road an eerie feel. The kids were grilling him. Why hadn't he gone and arrested all the skinheads in West Bromwich since they had expressed their intention of coming to Handsworth for a spot of Paki bashing?

It was a good question.

Unfortunately, his answer wasn't so good. An empty pint beer glass came sailing through the night and Superintendent Webb retired hurt. That was the riot in Handsworth. The skinheads never came, and a few hundred teenagers hung around for a while kicking in windows. There wasn't much on offer for looters because security advisers had visited all the video shops earlier in the day. Someone did break into the Mini Mart, but most of the nylon underpants and socks were left lying on the pavement because nobody wanted them, even for free. Later in the evening Special Patrol Group vans roamed the streets while on the frontline a handful of activists and late-night revellers hurled bricks at passing police vehicles. Of course some people did get hurt, but this wasn't a real riot: it lacked that kind of conviction. Too many people stayed home and watched it on television. Someone pressed a leaflet into John's hand as we were about to drive away in the early hours of Saturday morning. It said: 'Today's Pigs, Tomorrow's Bacon' and gave instructions about setting fire to and otherwise maiming policemen. It was a sick joke, because even if burning policemen was the answer, you weren't going to find it happening here. Handsworth had outgrown the ghetto in flames image. One of the clubs on the frontline even telephoned Thornhill Road and invited the police round for a drink to show there were no hard feelings.

On Saturday morning, the Bishop of Birmingham and a posse of photographers toured the riot area. It was OK, the buildings were still standing. Everyone blew a sigh of relief.

The nightmare that had seemed only too plausible a few years before had been avoided. The summer of 1976, in particular, had been unusually hot and oppressive. The weather seemed to mirror people's minds and provided the ideal climate for a moral panic. Down Westminster Road the sound systems were thumping away in the early hours, night after night. 'Man, yuh need an earplug to walk down de road sometime. Dem playing Niabinghi style, dat mean to say "death to all downpressors". Niabinghi men dem-a warriors, dem deal wid upfulness and pure righteousness. Dem-a holy warriors, y'unnerstand?'

In 1976, though, the holy warriors were better known as muggers – they had become the media's favourite folk devil, and mugging stories multiplied. Muggers always seemed to be young, male and, most importantly, Black. Every Black kid on the streets, therefore, was a potential mugger. Look at the way they stand around, watching, staring . . .

The relentless publicity given to street crime fed prejudices and distorted perceptions. At night the panda cars from Thornhill Road buzzed around: it seemed as if policemen were afraid to walk the streets any more. Instead, they were on line and plugged in, programmed to drive everywhere in second gear with blue lights flashing, looking for muggers.

Nineteen hundred and seventy-six was most definitely a time for the soothsayers, a year of portents and omens. Frightened JPs warned of extremists, Pentecostal preachers warned of race riots, and everywhere Rastas warned of war, a war that would go hot inna Babylon. In this way Handsworth became the new buzz word. So many sociologists came to examine the situation that one vicar put a sign outside his church saying 'Handsworth is not a zoo.'

The most articulate voice, though, came not from the outsiders, but from the residents. Carlton Green, a bus driver during the day, set out by night to collect Black residents' views on the police. For several months he toured youth clubs, pubs, homes and churches, setting up his tape and just telling people to sound off on their own wavelength. The sheer volume of bad feeling towards the police on Carlton's tapes staggered even those who thought they knew how bad the situation was. The tape transcripts fill two box files in the Waites Library in Lozells, Birmingham, and by the time an edited version of them, *Talking Blues*, was published in 1977, even the police had begun to acknowledge that silencing the holy warriors from Westminster Road was just the tip of the iceberg.

The story of police policy in Handsworth thus became the saga of how the police set about rehabilitating themselves. To start with it was called the community policing experiment and, under Superintendent David Webb, Handsworth became a regular watering hole for policemen from all over the world. Webb would show the visitors a selection of carefully nurtured contacts and a new image of mutual tolerance and understanding flowered. What was less obvious at the time, but which under Webb's successor Martin Burton has emerged as the crucial element in the new policy, is the role of the police in relation to other services. This link with probation, education, housing and social services is now referred to officially as the 'Corporate Approach'. Martin Burton scoffs at the fancy title and calls it 'good, old-fashioned coppering'.

Whatever you call it, the effect has been to draw the police more and more into the inner city rescue act. Their influence and advice has affected housing policies, for example, particularly in relation to young Black people. This may be good old-fashioned coppering as far as Burton is concerned, but it is light years away from Dixon of Dock Green. And with the advent of the Lozells project, the police have, albeit indirectly, gained influence over a tidy sum of inner city partnership money for projects which benefit police – community relations. The fact that this has been used, amongst other things, to help equip and set up a sound system – one of the alleged causes of trouble in the first place – is a most pleasing and revealing irony.

In fact the riot leaflet should have said: 'Today's Pigs, Tomorrow's Politicians', because the police are much more conscious of protocol now. But then, so are the holy warriors. In the old days, one group called Jungleman used to favour direct action – like throwing typewriters through windows – to get what they wanted. The police knew their way to Jungleman's house blindfold.

Then, in the Enlightenment, people listened more to what they were saying. The local housing association found them a big house where they wouldn't disturb the neighbours and a trust fund helped them to buy a van to transport their sound system. Now Jungleman are positively respectable, aside from the occasional ganga bust. But they are coming to the end of the gravy train. One member of Jungleman came to discuss his plans for raising money to tour the sound system in Ghana. He had spent a considerable time in Accra the previous year arranging venues, getting the right permits from the Ministry of Culture, and signing agreements with the Ghanaian Musicians' Union. He had armfuls of concertina files stuffed with papers and documents. He looked depressed. To transport the sound equipment, the van and the nine members of the group to Ghana was going to cost at least £15,000. A couple of months previously he had sent out 485 appeals to trust funds setting out the aims and ideals of Jungleman's umbrella organisation, Exodus. Only three replies looked favourable and the donations amounted to just over £1,000.

I looked at the pile of 'sorry we can't help you this time' and thought about the effort that must have gone into sending out those 485 appeals. Just hustling the photocopies alone must have been a major task. 'Wouldn't it be easier to knock over a post office?' I said. 'Oh man, don't say that. That's what I get from the other brothers all the time.'

Brian was riding his cousin's new bicycle through Handsworth when he was stopped by police, taken to the police station and questioned for half an hour about where he got the bike. 'They started to thump me. I know the real reason was not 'cos they thought I stole the bike but because I was Black. We are regarded as lower than animals in the eyes of the white man.' Extract from *Talking Blues*, published in 1977.

Squats, noise, mugging and drugs – the media stereotype of Handsworth in the late 1970s

Myrtle Edwards, a Jamaican-born hospital worker, and her two sons were arrested and charged with assaulting two young policemen who had stopped one of the sons and tried to take him away on a suspected burglary charge. It was a simple case of mistaken identity, but the police didn't check. A Bank Holiday crowd gathered and a fight broke out. The policemen were left unconscious in the street. In court the judge criticised them because they had broken just about every rule in the book and provoked a near riot. But he told Mrs Edwards: 'Two policemen have been injured and someone must pay.' All three members of the family received six-month custodial sentences. Mrs Edwards said after leaving prison: 'The Lord knows I am innocent, and I leave it to the Lord to deal with the wicked.'

In November 1980 Stephen Thompson was transferred from prison to Rampton Hospital seven days before his expected release date. Home Office officials had decided that Stephen's conversion to the Rastafarian faith and the writings and drawings he subsequently produced indicated 'a schizophrenic condition'. William Whitelaw, Home Secretary at the time, admitted in a confidential letter to Stephen's MP: 'It has been suggested that difficulties can arise when white psychiatrists who know little about the cultural background of ethnic minorities attempt to assess the state of mental health of someone with this background . . .'

Ronald Jeffers (*right*) was transferred from Stafford to Lincoln Prison after a riot over food. Jeffers claimed he was forced to eat pork. At Lincoln he went on hunger strike and after five weeks he was taken to hospital suffering from starvation and dehydration. He needed an emergency operation and kidney dialysis treatment to save his life. He was also suffering from knee and arm injuries, and his legs and buttocks were covered in sores. He claims he was beaten and drugged. The Home Secretary was asked how a prisoner could get into such a condition. In his reply William Whitelaw said: 'I have found the allegations [by Jeffers] to be groundless.'

Dave Butchere (*above in conversation with Webb*) was arrested by Special Patrol Group officers in a Lozells service station. They searched his van and found a rounders bat and a small metal tool. He was charged with carrying offensive weapons. Mr Butchere, who works with homeless young people, was cleared in court. In a local radio interview Superintendent David Webb (*opposite, sitting*) was asked if there was an anti-police feeling amongst immigrant communities. He replied: 'Absolutely

not. Just the reverse. We've got a
tremendous rapport with the local
community because we've all got a
vested interest in the place.' He
resigned from the police force in 1981,
protesting about the lack of national
interest in community policing. 'I feel
that for several years I have been
banging my head against a brick wall,'
he said. He subsequently went into the
import-export business.

Handsworth Park, 1981. Martin Burton, who became Superintendent following Webb's resignation, takes the platform at a Krishna rally.

Soho Road, July 11th 1981. 'Future
historians may well say that the nation's
battle for policing a multiracial society
by consent was won on Soho Road and
in the backstreets of Handsworth.' –
Lord Scarman

Placard text: ANGUS. WILLIAMS GLENFORD. REID. OSSIE. CAMERON SELF. DEFENCE. NO. OFFENCE.

GLENFORD REID BEATEN & FRAMED BY HANDSWORTHS RACIST COMMUNITY POLICE DAVE BUTCHER ACTION COMMITTEE

DAVE
BUTCHER
FRAMED
BY SPG
NO CASE
TO ANSWER

COMMUNITY
POLICING =
BRUTALITY
+
FRAME UP

STUFF
COMMUNITY
POLICING

STOP THE
CRIMINALISATION
OF BLACK PEOPLE

The 'Corporate Approach' was launched in February 1983 when a public meeting (*above*) was held to encourage community participation in the Lozells project, an experimental policing scheme jointly supported by the education, probation and social services. The project has an annual budget of £50,000 to distribute to schemes which enable the police to develop closer links with the community. The police have also consolidated traditional links with schools.

Right, a beat bobby stands trial in a classroom court.

PC Terry Underhill on beat seventeen, Handsworth, 1984.

SS JESUS

Backstage a furious discussion about religion was taking place. A trim God-squadder in a smart black suit and neat Afro hairstyle was haranguing Peter Tosh, the Jamaican reggae singer. Tosh, stripped to the waist and surrounded by awestruck acolytes, was busy pushing an eighth of an ounce of hash into a little pipe. The God-squadder was out of place, but determined to have his say. 'Do you believe in the ways of the Lord?' he persisted, in a high-pitched Liverpudlian accent. 'I believe in the Lord of Lords,' Tosh informed him, between puffs on his pipe. 'Do you believe in Jesus?' continued the God-squadder, now partly obscured by the sickly-sweet clouds of smoke issuing from Tosh's pipe. Several dreadlocked brethren pulled at his sleeve, indicating that he might do well to step outside the dressing room. 'Jesus!' Tosh snorted with derision. 'Jesus is a boat, the SS *Jesus*.' Guffaws accompanied the God-squadder's exit, but from the corridor came his parting shot: 'Yes, but couldn't a lot of people sail on by to salvation in His boat?'

The question was lost in the laughter, but it deserved an answer: there are, after all, so many people seeking salvation. And the desperate energy of their search has sustained Handsworth's most spectacular growth industry over the past twenty years – church building. Pentecostal halls, Sikh *gurdwaras*, Rastafarian groundations, a Hindu temple, Buddhist centres, a Jain Ashram, Muslim prayer houses and a mosque have become the culture focus for the area.

It's not just the Christians who are in the boat-building business. The whole community is looking for a spiritual life raft.

The reasons are not hard to find. Sometimes you come face to face with them. Jagat Singh, for example, has been convicted on drunk and disorderly charges more than 300 times. Once he was arrested for being drunk sixty-three minutes after being released from Winson Green prison – where he had just served two weeks because he was unable to pay the fine from his previous drunk and disorderly conviction. Jagat has never stolen anything or hurt anyone – he just gets drunk, all the time. He started drinking in 1966, two and a half years after first coming to work in Britain. Like many of his fellow countrymen, he spent all day sweating in a foundry, and like many others found welcome relaxation in the pub after work. For the first two years he worked hard, but then he just broke apart. And no one could put him back together again. Not the police, nor the Drug Addiction Unit at All Saints' Hospital, nor the warders at the prison; not even the Smethwick *gurdwara* where people's physical needs are often catered for. Jagat served in the British Army in India, and his proud military bearing is something that not even seventeen years of cheap sherry can completely wash away. But he remains a mystery, a folk legend whose exploits span the emotions from sublime comedy to darkest tragedy. The kids in the high street giggle when he starts directing the traffic, but the older Punjabis cannot laugh: they can hardly bear to look. Jagat's disintegration is their personal nightmare made flesh.

His story is not an isolated case. The nightmare is repeated over and over again in the files which pack the shelves of the advice centres clustered around Soho and Villa Road; in the Law Centre, the Asian Resource Centre, Harambee and many others. These are the unofficial histories of the Home Front, not the official statistics. They are histories so complex, so confusing and so painful that no one really knows how to begin telling them. Ranjit Sondhi, one of the workers at the Asian Resource Centre, once sat down and recalled for me what he had been doing that day. His case load had included a Pakistani man threatened with deportation because twenty years earlier his father had made a false tax declaration; a Punjabi who had suffered a severe industrial injury but was ignoring medical advice and returning to work early for fear of losing his job; a Bangladeshi with a child benefit problem; and a Sikh who, though in his seventies, was still signing on because when he came to Britain he had given his National Insurance age as less than his real one in order to be able to work as long as possible. Ranjit had also been asked to advise a girl with a Pakistani father, an Irish mother and a Jamaican husband, whom she now disliked, about the possibility of repatriation to Pakistan. 'I know, it's crazy,' he admitted. 'What can you say? I mean, going off to Pakistan when she can't speak the bloody language. But see it as a desperate attempt to escape from £200 rent arrears and a husband who beats her up . . .' In fact, see behind all those little indicators – like the growing number of Black people admitted to the local mental hospital or the visibly rising number of alcoholics on the streets – something of the real desperation on the Home Front. And desperation can breed a kind of fanatical power.

I first met Chan Singh Kalsi a few months after he had been made redundant from Wilmot Breedon, an engineering works. He was fifty-two and he was getting desperate. It wasn't just the redundancy notice, it was the sum of a lifetime of redundancy notices. Mr Kalsi was born in India and then taken to Kenya as a child by his father who had gone to help the British in the 1930s. He grew up as a businessman in Kenya and opened up a garage, but when independence came his garage went out of the window. The English Kenyans got compensation: Mr Kalsi got his marching orders. By 1972 he had established himself and his family in Uganda, but Idi Amin's rise to power forced him to flee once again. He arrived in England with his wife, four sons, and two daughters – and no money. They faced a wave of hostility whipped up by sensational headlines in the press. The family lived in two rooms of an Aston terrace during the winter of 1972, hardly able to do anything because of the cold. Eventually Mr Kalsi caught pneumonia. 'The doctor was angry,' he recalls. 'He kept swearing at me and my wife. I couldn't understand it. Everyone was so rude. The landlord kept telling the children to go back to the jungle. And when I walked down the street I couldn't understand why the kids kept calling me a "Paki bastard".' But he refused to give up. He finally got a job as a paint sprayer, and then an even better one as a production charge hand at Wilmot Breedon.

The next time I saw Mr Kalsi was four years later, and he was leading a procession to mark the opening of a new temple inspired by the Guru Darshan Singh Das. 'I don't know if this man has all the answers,' he said, 'but : . .' and he gestured towards the old junior school which had been transformed in a few short months to a busy, newly decorated religious centre. He gestured towards the sound of drumming and singing in the hall, the aroma of dahl and chapatis from the free kitchen, but, most importantly, towards the knowledge that, somehow, he had found a way of keeping his family secure. It was a convincing answer.

There is, however, one church that no one goes to any more. It stands, unloved and unlovely, just a few yards from the terrace where John and I have our darkroom in Grove Lane. It used to be the parish church. The Queen signed the papers making it redundant in 1978 – it had been years since anyone had used the place. At first glance it looks like a prima facie case of negligence on the part of the vicar. Lost: in Handsworth, one flock. Please return to fold. But sitting in the vicarage, surrounded by bookshelves like sandbags of theology, a more telling tale emerges. John Faulds moved to Handsworth in 1969, only to find some of his new parishioners confronting him with his past crimes – had he not opened up his home to Black people and other undesirables? His response did not satisfy them, and his pews emptied, rapidly.

But it was perhaps only then that he could begin to know his parish. Once, John Faulds invited the Bishop of Birmingham to meet some of his parishioners – a Punjabi family. Everyone sat around eating samosas in the front room making stilted conversation for a while until one man suddenly blurted out: 'Why are you trying to get rid of our vicar?' The Bishop looked a little disconcerted. The man pressed on. He wanted a categorical assurance that 'our vicar' was not going to get the sack. John Faulds looked very embarrassed. The bishop choked on his samosa. What was a Sikh doing cross-examining the Bishop of Birmingham? This was taking interfaith dialogue too far. He fled into the night saying: 'I refuse to be harassed like this.' John Faulds remains, but the Bishop is not happy. 'Our vicar' raises too many theological problems. 'You must remember,' he once said to me, 'I have no Brownie pack and it is many a long year since the Mothers' Union met. These are grievous crimes . . .'

In 1980 Dang Van Thu and his family spent weeks drifting in the South China Sea after becoming refugees from North Vietnam. In the foreground is a model of the boat that brought them to 'freedom', made by the family while staying in a reception centre. In spite of attempts by Home Office-funded resettlement groups to disperse the Vietnamese refugees around the country, many families – like the Dangs – have been drawn to Handsworth where there is a pastoral centre run by another refugee, the Roman Catholic priest Father Peter Diem.

133

AK NAAM CHARDI KALA
BHANE ARB DA BHAL

Left, a procession to mark the opening of the Sachkhand Nanak Dham (SND) temple which has been housed in a former Church junior school. *Above*, Ravi Dass temple, Handsworth – the first low caste *gurdwara* to open in Britain. The building was converted from a Methodist chapel.

Above, the Good News Asian Church, which opened in August 1983, was the first Christian/Asian to be established by an Asian congregation outside India. The services are conducted from an Alternative Service book in either English, Urdu or Punjabi – depending on the congregation.

Opposite page, top, the Bishop of Birmingham, the Right Reverend Hugh Montefiore, on his way to consecrate the Good News Asian Church. *Left*, consecrating the ground of the new SND temple.
Overleaf, Birmingham Central Mosque, the first to be built in Britain.

Above, the Guru Nanak Nishkan Sewak Jatha *gurdwara*. *Left*, the Life and Light Fellowship. *Right*, Ethiopian Orthodox Church.

Above, Vietnamese New Year
celebrations, Saint Francis Centre,
1984.

Mother tongue teaching has become an important adjunct to most religious centres in Handsworth. *Far left*, Vietnamese children are given lessons in Vietnamese history and culture. *Left*, Punjabi classes, Smethwick *gurdwara*. *Above*, the concern felt by many Afro-Caribbean parents about their children's performance in state schools has led many Black churches to open supplementary classes at weekends.

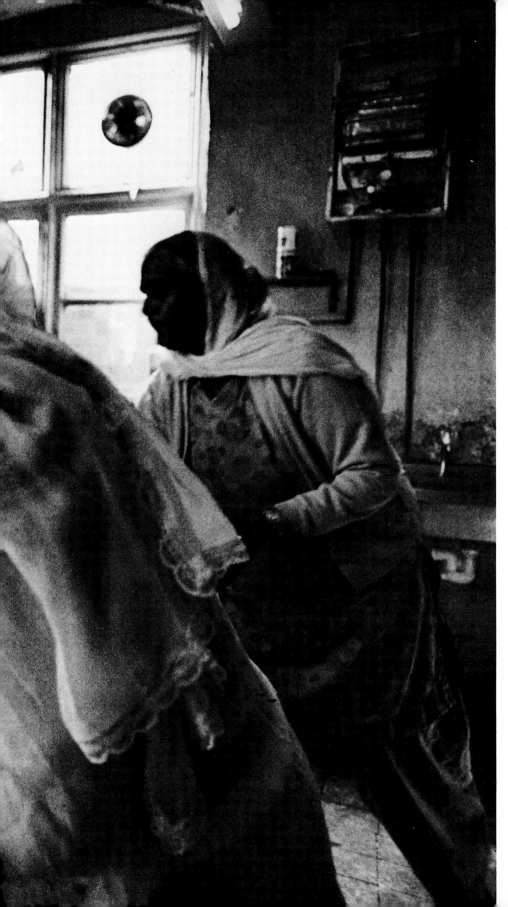

Left, chapattis being made at
Smethwick *gurdwara* for the *langa* (free
kitchen), 1982.
Above, Meals on Wheels, Handsworth,
1982.

Left, the Ethiopian World Federation was set up to lobby support for Ethiopia during the Italian invasion of 1935. It is one of several Rastafarian organisations active in Handsworth and was instrumental in helping the first Rastas to return to Ethiopia during the 1960s.

Above, a speaker at a Sikh meeting held in Handsworth to protest about a Birmingham headmaster's refusal to allow one of his pupils to attend school wearing a turban. More than 40,000 people marched on 10 Downing Street following the meeting.

Hosannah '79 in Handsworth Park featured ex-Black Panther Eldridge Cleaver and Cliff Richard. Cleaver told the crowd: 'Yes, I've sold out. I've sold out to Jesus, and it's the best bargain I've ever made.'

ACKNOWLEDGMENTS

The authors wish to acknowledge financial help from West Midlands Arts and, in the production of this book, from the Arts Council of Great Britain.

Our sincere thanks to the many people who have helped and advised in making this book, and in particular: Brian Homer, Alan Hughes, Linda MacFadyen, Merrise Crooks, Margot Wilkes, Lu Hersey, *Ten 8* magazine, Neville Reid, Ranjit Sondhi, and Bindi Kalsi.

Photographs on pages 68, 70 and 71 are reproduced with the kind permission of *The Times*. The photograph on page 80 is reproduced with the kind permission of the *Observer*.

Photographs on pages 29, 32, 46, 49, 50, 51, 61, 75, 78, 88, 93, 107, 113, 116, 141 and 149 are by Derek Bishton. The remaining photographs are by John Reardon.